Barbie™
YOU CAN BE
5-MINUTE STORIES

5 - MINUTE STORIES

Published in the United States by Random House Children's Books, a division of Penguin Random House LLC,
1745 Broadway, New York, NY 10019, and in Canada by Penguin Random House Canada Limited, Toronto.
Random House and the colophon are registered trademarks of Penguin Random House LLC.

Visit us on the Web!
randomhousekids.com

Educators and librarians, for a variety of teaching tools, visit us at RHTeacherLibrarians.com

ISBN 978-1-5247-1505-2

MANUFACTURED IN CHINA

10 9 8 7 6 5 4 3 2 1

CONTENTS

5-MINUTE STORIES

Random House 🏠 New York

YOU CAN BE

A CHEF

One Saturday, Barbie and Nikki visited their favorite food truck, Chef Halle's Fancy Mac.

"Mmmmm!" Barbie said, taking a big bite of her macaroni and cheese. "This is so delicious!"

Barbie's best friend, Nikki, agreed. "Chef Halle's Fancy Mac is the best!" she exclaimed.

"It's so sweet and creamy. And I think I taste garlic, too," Barbie guessed.

"You know what?" Barbie said suddenly. "I'm going to make Fancy Mac for us tomorrow!"

Nikki's eyes twinkled. "Yum! Count me in. I'll bring Teresa!"

At the grocery story the next morning, Barbie looked at the different cheeses. There were so many!

Hmm. Which one does Chef Halle use? she wondered.

After a while, she chose Roquefort cheese, which sounded very fancy!

At home, Barbie scrunched her nose and said, "This cheese smells really strong. Maybe I picked the wrong one." She glanced up at the clock. Her friends would be over soon. There was still a lot to do!

"Maybe when I mix in the milk, the cheese won't be so smelly," she said hopefully, and set the timer.

When Nikki and Teresa arrived, they couldn't wait to taste Barbie's Fancy Mac.

Teresa tried hers first. "Mmm, creamy," she said. Then she stopped smiling.

Nikki tasted a forkful, too. "It's ... it's ... nice," she said unconvincingly.

"What? It's not good?" Barbie asked.

"No—it's fine, Barbie," Teresa said, trying to smile. "It's . . . interesting."

Barbie took a bite and spit it out immediately. "This isn't interesting—this is terrible!"

"It's not that bad, Barbie," Teresa said. "I mean, it's really creamy. Maybe you just used the wrong cheese or something?"

Barbie nodded. "There's more to cooking than I thought. Tomorrow I'm going to ask Chef Halle if she'll teach me how to make her Fancy Mac!"

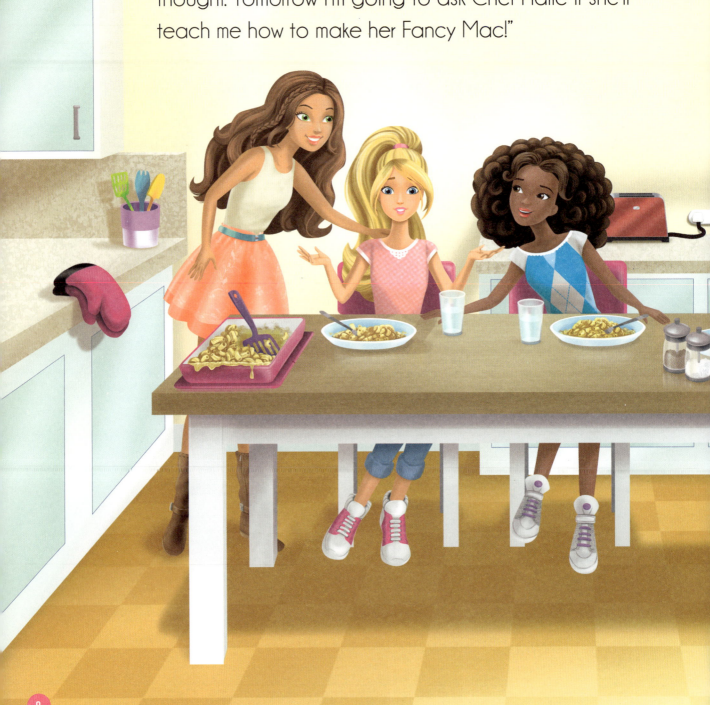

The next day, Barbie explained to Chef Halle how her Fancy Mac had been a failure.

"You used Roquefort cheese?" the chef asked, surprised. "A cheese with a fancy name isn't what makes my Fancy Mac so good."

"What does, then?" Barbie asked.

"If you come by the Horizons Senior Center, where I volunteer as a chef, I'll teach you the recipe," Chef Halle said.

"That would be amazing!" said Barbie. "Thank you!"

The next day, Barbie stood in Chef Halle's busy kitchen at the senior center. She was ready to start making delicious Fancy Mac.

Barbie grabbed a wooden spoon from the counter. "All set!" she exclaimed.

"Not so fast," Chef Halle told her. "Before you cook, bake, chop, dice, or boil anything in my kitchen, you need to learn Chef Halle's Kitchen Rules." She pointed to a sign that hung above the ovens.

Barbie studied the sign carefully. She saw that the rules were created to keep everyone in the kitchen safe.

That night, Barbie went over Chef Halle's Kitchen Rules in her head. Then she read through the list of ingredients in the Fancy Mac recipe until she came to the words *spinach* and *onions*.

"Spinach and onions?" she said . "That's strange. I don't remember tasting spinach or onions."

Then the recipe listed one bay leaf.

"And I'm pretty sure I've never seen a bay leaf in Chef Halle's Fancy Mac!" Barbie said.

When she felt she knew the recipe by heart, she slipped the card back into her bag and turned off the light.

The next day, Barbie recited all the rules to Chef Halle.

"Very good," said the chef. "Here are the ingredients for the Fancy Mac. Do you remember what we do first?"

Barbie smiled. "We boil water for the pasta," she announced confidently.

"Are you sure?" Chef Halle asked. "It's okay if you need to look at the recipe."

Barbie shook her head. "That's okay. I know it," she replied. "Wait!" she cried. "First we preheat the oven! *Then* we boil the water."

Chef Halle grinned and motioned for Barbie to start.

"Preheating the oven!"
Barbie called out excitedly.

"Boiling the water
for the pasta!" Barbie
announced next.

"Measuring the ingredients!
Greasing the baking dishes!"

Barbie felt like a real chef as she worked next to
Chef Halle and her assistants in the kitchen.
She stirred pasta in the enormous pot.
"Careful!" Barbie said. "Hot pot coming through!"

Barbie's favorite part of cooking was chopping the onions, even though the strong fumes made her eyes tear up!

"Do I look like I'm crying?" she asked through her tears.

"Yes, you do!" Chef Halle replied with a laugh.

Chef Halle asked, "What's the next step?"

"I memorized the recipe last night," Barbie said.

"Barbie, you don't need to memorize the recipes," Chef Halle told her. "Cooking is about taking your time and checking your steps along the way. Even I keep my recipes right here in my apron pocket. Now, take a peek at your recipe and see what's next."

Barbie relaxed and read the card. "It's time to add the cheese!" she announced. She and Assistant Chef Allison added it to the pasta, poured the mixture into baking dishes, and sprinkled breadcrumbs on top.

"It's ready to go in the oven!" Barbie announced.

"Are you sure?" asked Chef Halle.

Barbie checked her recipe card. "I'm sure!" she replied.

"That smells delicious, Barbie," Chef Halle said when they pulled the trays of Fancy Mac from the oven.

"Thanks!" Barbie replied. "And this time it looks just like yours."

"Let's head into the dining room, then," Chef Halle said, "and see if it tastes as good as it looks!"

"Surprise!" Barbie's friends shouted when she stepped into the dining room.

Barbie gasped. "What are you guys doing here?"

"Chef Halle invited us," Nikki told her.

"We can't wait to try your Fancy Mac!" said Teresa.

Barbie held her breath as everyone took a bite.

"This tastes amazing, Barbie!" exclaimed Nikki.

Just then, Raquelle, who was also volunteering at the senior center, appeared at her table. "What's this Fancy Mac everyone keeps raving about?" she asked.

"Why don't you try it for yourself," replied Barbie.

Raquelle took a bite of the mac and cheese and smiled. "Mmmmm," she said, and stopped.

"What is it, Raquelle?" Barbie asked.

Raquelle slowly opened her mouth . . . and pulled out a bay leaf!

"Oh, no!" Barbie cried. "I forgot to take out the bay leaf!"

Chef Halle leaned in and whispered, "No worries, Barbie. That happens to professional chefs, too—myself included!"

Barbie laughed. "Step nine," she read from the card, "says 'Remove the bay leaf'!"

"You can be a great chef!" said Chef Halle.

Dear Chef Halle,

    It was SO much fun learning how to make Fancy Mac with you at the senior center! I can't believe how much there is to know about being a chef.

    Thank you for everything you taught me. Maybe you can show me how to cut onions without crying (ha ha)! And I promise—the next time I make Fancy Mac, I'll remember to take out the bay leaf!

Your friend,
Barbie

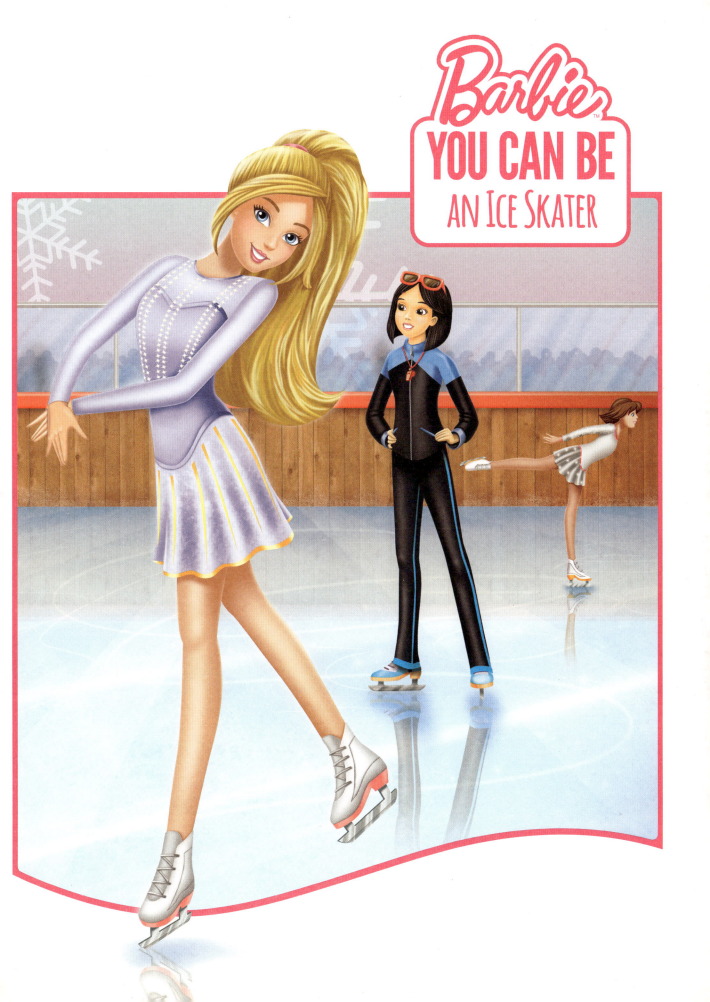

Barbie™

YOU CAN BE
an Ice Skater

On a clear, crisp winter day, Barbie carefully laced up her new ice skates. She couldn't wait to get out onto the ice.

"Over here, Barbie!" called Teresa.

"Ooooh, nice skates!" said Summer.

"They feel great," said Barbie. "My old ones were too small."

Suddenly, Teresa lost her balance and grabbed onto Barbie. They tumbled to the ice, laughing.

"Are you guys okay?" asked Summer.

"Yeah," said Teresa. "Sorry, Barbie."

"No problem," Barbie replied. "Falling is kind of fun when you're with friends!"

Later, Barbie decided to try a Bunny Hop jump. She skated down the ice, brought her right leg back, swung it forward, and hopped into the air. She landed and kept going.

Summer and Teresa gave their friend two thumbs up!

A woman skated up to Barbie and introduced herself.

"My name is Mai Liou, and I'm the new coach of the figure-skating club," she said. "Ever thought about joining?"

"Am I qualified?" Barbie asked.

"We take skaters of all levels," explained Coach Mai. "Stop by the indoor rink tomorrow at four if you're interested."

Barbie told her friends what the coach had said.

"How exciting," said Teresa, holding tightly to the railing. "Are you going to check it out?"

"Maybe," said Barbie, imagining skating in front of a packed crowd. "I need to think about it."

The rest of the afternoon, Barbie practiced her skating moves. Then she saw another skater go into a sit spin. "I wish I could do that," she said.

"Sounds like you're going for it," said Summer.

Barbie smiled. "I think I am!"

The next day, Barbie arrived at the ice rink a little
nervous but excited to get started. She quickly found
Coach Mai, who was watching the skaters warm up.
"I'm ready to begin!" Barbie said.

"Well, you're off to a good start," said the coach. "Rule number one is to be on time to every practice so you don't miss anything. Only skaters who are on time will get to skate in the shows."

"Got it!" Barbie said enthusiastically.

Barbie could hardly wait to get on the ice!

Coach Mai introduced Barbie to another skater, named Matt. "You two are at about the same level," the coach said. "And you're both dressed correctly for practice."

The coach pointed to her own outfit. "Warm clothing, of course. Stretchy pants. And gloves to protect your hands when you fall."

Coach Mai announced that the club would be putting on its Winter Wonderland Ice Show in a few weeks. Barbie wanted to be ready!

She learned all about the edges on skates: outside edges point away from the body; inside edges point toward the body.

Coach Mai also spent a lot of time on the right way to fall. "Try not to use your hands to break a fall. You can hurt your wrists. And if you feel that you're about to fall, bend your knees and squat down."

Barbie learned how to skate backward, too. She practiced and practiced.

The week of the Winter Wonderland Ice Show, Barbie got a call from Teresa. She wanted to know what time to arrive for Barbie's skating performance.

Barbie was telling Teresa all about learning to skate backward when she checked the time. Practice was starting, and Barbie was going to be late!

When Barbie finally got to practice, she apologized to Coach Mai for being late.

The coach listened patiently but explained that Barbie had missed some important information.

"I'm sorry, Barbie," she said, "but I can't let you skate in the ice show. It wouldn't be fair to my other students."

"I understand," said Barbie sadly. "I'm sorry. It won't happen again."

On the day of the show, Summer could tell Barbie felt bad that she wasn't skating.

"I missed something really important when I was late for practice," Barbie told Summer. "I don't know if I can catch up by the next show."

"You can do it. I know you can," said Summer. "You just have to put in some extra practice time."

By the next practice, Barbie had set a goal for herself. She wanted to be able to do a sit spin at the next show. "I almost did it that time," said Barbie. "But I don't know if I'll ever get it right."

"You're doing great," Coach Mai encouraged her. "As long as you keep practicing, you'll get it. It took me a few weeks to do my first sit spin."

After a few more tries . . . "I did it!" Barbie exclaimed proudly. "That felt great!"

"Congratulations!" said Coach Mai. "Now do it again, just like that—about a million times!"

"Sure," Barbie said, smiling. "No problem!"

Barbie put in extra practice time at the outdoor rink. "Let's see what you've been working on," said Summer. "Okay, watch this," Barbie said. She skated off and started gaining speed. Everything felt right, but as Barbie went into her sit spin, she fell.

"Are you okay?" asked Summer.

"I'm fine," said Barbie, getting up. "I'm not sure what happened. I thought I had this."

"Don't worry," said Teresa. "You'll get it."

But the ice show was tomorrow, and Barbie felt a little nervous.

The next day, Coach Mai called the student skaters together.

"Each of you has the skills you need to perform your routines. So take a deep breath and relax," she said. "All that really matters is that you go out there, do your best, and have fun!"

Barbie waited for her turn to skate.

"Great job!" Barbie told Matt as he came off the ice.

"Thanks, Barbie," he replied. "Good luck."

Barbie took a deep breath. She was next.

Barbie felt good as she glided onto the ice. She skated on the inside and outside edges, crossing over on the turns, and ended with a short Bunny Hop.

Then Barbie moved smoothly into skating backward.

"Go for it!" cheered Summer and Teresa. "Do the sit spin!"

Barbie came out of her backward skate and swung her right leg forward to begin the spin. She settled into a sitting position, bending her left leg and extending her arms in a diamond shape.

"I did it!" exclaimed Barbie.

"You can be a great ice skater," said Coach Mai proudly.

Dear Coach Mai,

Thank you so much for encouraging me to join the ice skating club! I learned so much, and I'm so excited I can do a sit spin. Now I'm ready to set my next goal and start practicing a triple axle. Or maybe I'll stick to a toe loop to start.

Your friend,
Barbie

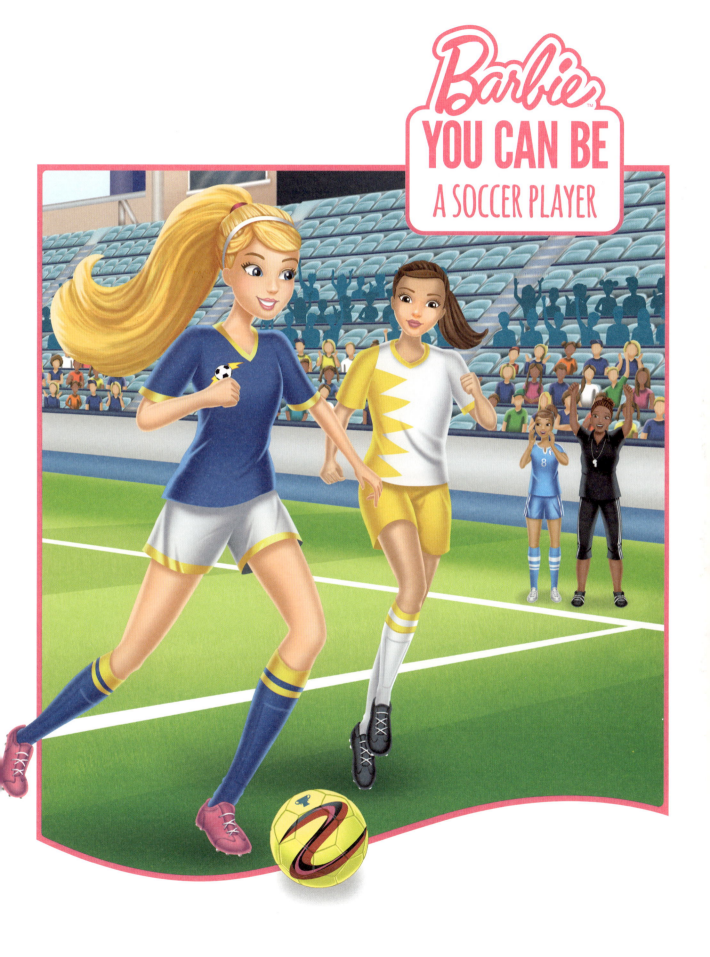

It was Saturday, and Barbie had a big soccer game that afternoon. Her team, Avalanche, was in the semifinals. The winner of today's game would get to play in the championships at a real professional soccer stadium.

Barbie's younger sister Stacie handed Barbie her
shin guards. "I really hope your team wins!" she said.
Barbie packed up her cleats. "Me too! And I hope these
cleats help me with my corner kick. I can't seem to get it right."

Barbie arrived at the field for practice before the game. Barbie, Nikki, and Raquelle were in charge of leading the team in stretching and warm-up drills before every game.

As they warmed up, an older girl walked onto the field.

"You're Lucy Rose!" Barbie said excitedly. "From the Malibu Wave Crashers!"

"Lucy is going to train with us before the game today," Barbie's coach, Jordyn, told them. "And she will co-coach with me during the game."

Barbie and her friends were so excited.

The game started, and the Avalanche team
was doing well. Barbie raced toward the goal.
Nobody from the other team was guarding her.
"Raquelle!" she cried. "I'm open!"

"Pass to Barbie!" Lucy called from the sidelines.

"Barbie is open!" Coach Jordyn called.

But Raquelle ignored them. She dribbled the ball down the field until a defender was right in front of her. Raquelle kicked the ball, but it went out of bounds, far from the net.

"Why didn't you pass it to me?" Barbie asked. Raquelle shrugged. "I thought I had it."

The referee blew the whistle when the first half of the game was over.

"Great job, everyone!" Coach Jordyn told them as they drank from their water bottles. "In the next half, let's have some more passing."

Barbie looked at Raquelle to see if she was listening. But Raquelle was busy fixing her ponytail.

In the second half, Raquelle still did not pass the ball.

"I'm open!" Nikki yelled.

But Raquelle pretended not to hear her. Finally, with a few minutes left in the game, the other team kicked the ball out of bounds. That meant the Avalanche team had a corner kick.

"Barbie!" Coach Jordyn called. "Take the kick!"

The second her foot touched the ball, Barbie knew it was a bad kick. She frowned as she watched the ball fly out of bounds.

"It's okay!" shouted Lucy Rose. "The game's not over yet!"

Lucy was right. Barbie shook off the bad kick and ran onto the field.

With just one minute left, Megan raced toward the net. "Raquelle! *I'm open!*" she cried.

But Raquelle kept charging toward the net. Even though two players from the other team were covering her closely, Raquelle took the shot. She scored!

The whistle blew and the game was over. It was close, but the Avalanche team had won!

"We're in the finals!" Nikki cheered.

"Thanks to me!" Raquelle exclaimed.

"This was a team win," Coach Jordyn corrected her. "One person didn't win this game. Team Avalanche won this game."

"Great game, girls!" Lucy told them. "To prepare for the championship, how would you like to come to the Malibu Wave Crashers Stadium and practice with the team?"

"Yes!" they cheered.

Before she left, Barbie asked Lucy if she could help her with her corner kick.

Lucy smiled. "Sure! Why don't you come to the stadium?"

"Wow!" exclaimed Barbie. "That would be great!"

The next day, Barbie was so excited.

Lucy helped Barbie set up a corner kick. "Count out your steps in your head," she said. "Keep your head up. Look at your teammates waiting at the net. Then kick to the player you think the goalie isn't watching."

Barbie looked out at the goal. Her teammates for the drill were ready.

Barbie counted three steps toward the ball and kicked it hard. The ball sailed through the air, right to Emily. Emily kicked it past the goalie and into the net.

"That's it!" Lucy cheered.

Soon Barbie's teammates arrived at the stadium for practice.

"You want to put yourself in the perfect spot to receive the ball," Lucy told the girls. "Barbie, stand by the goalpost and show everybody the spot I told you about. When Raquelle passes you the ball, turn left and shoot!"

"What's the point of passing?" Raquelle objected.
"I can score from here!"

"You won't always have the best shot, Raquelle,"
Lucy said. "Always listen for your teammates. Then look
to see who is open and pass to that player."

"Okay, okay," Raquelle muttered under her breath.

The girls started their game. Soon Barbie found herself in the perfect spot to score. "I'm open!" she yelled.

But Raquelle ignored her. She moved closer to the goal and prepared to shoot the ball herself. That was when another player snuck in and stole the ball away.

"Megan, sub for Raquelle!" Coach Jordyn called. Raquelle stomped off the field.

Later, with seconds left in the game, Coach Jordyn put Raquelle back in. Team Avalanche caught a lucky break when the other team kicked the ball out of bounds. It was a corner kick for the Avalanche team!

Coach Jordyn asked Barbie to take the kick.

Focus! Barbie told herself.

Count out your steps.

Play with your head up.

Look for your teammates.

She set the ball down and checked to see who was open.

The only person open was . . . Raquelle.

Barbie kicked the ball to Raquelle as hard as she could. But when it fell at Raquelle's feet, the other team had already moved to block her from the goal.

"Pass to Nikki!" Barbie called.

Raquelle frowned. Barbie could tell she wanted to take the shot herself. But she passed the ball to Nikki anyway.

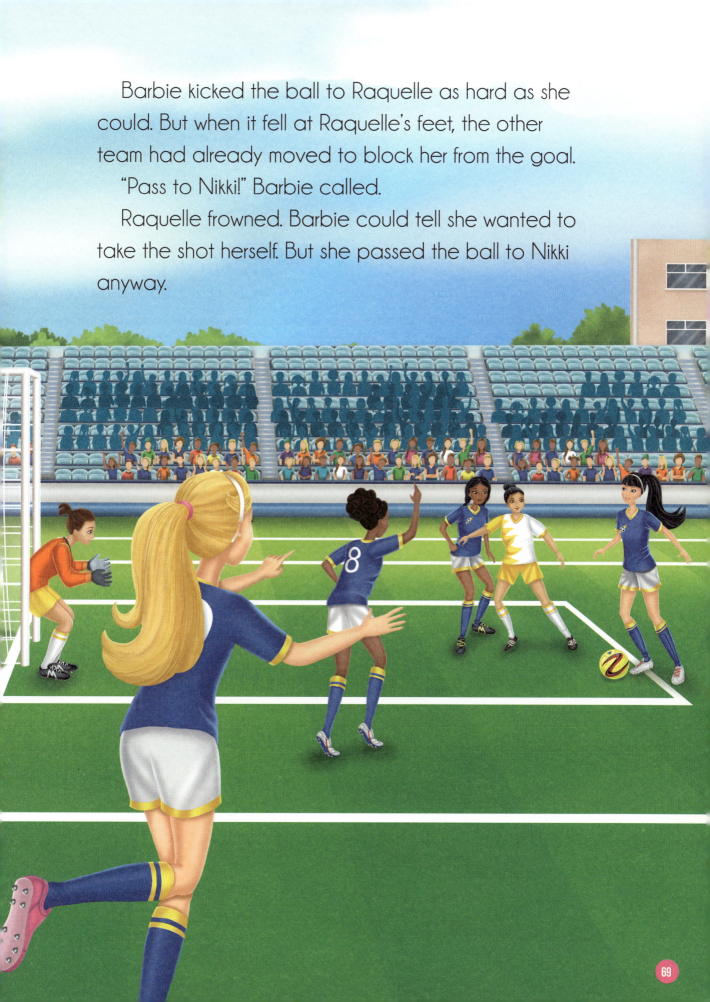

Nikki settled the ball, then punted it into the
net just as the whistle blew to end the game.
Team Avalanche had won!

Barbie's teammates raced onto the field. Everyone was cheering and hugging each other.

"Great goal, Nikki!" Coach Jordyn cried.

"Awesome corner kick, Barbie!" Lucy cheered.

Barbie grabbed Raquelle's hand and raised it in the air. "And an amazing assist from Raquelle!" Barbie added. "This win really was a team effort!"

"You can bc a grcat soccer player," Lucy said.

Dear Lucy,

   I still can't believe we won the championship!
Thank you so much for training with our team
and for helping me with my corner kick. I felt
like a real Wave Crasher when I took that kick.
And Raquelle's assist to Nikki was amazing!
You taught all of us what it really means to play
as a team.

   Your friend,
   Barbie

Barbie was so excited! She was going to spend the day volunteering at her childhood pediatrician's office.

Her favorite nurse, Mira, asked Barbie to sit in the waiting room until the doctor was ready for her to get started.

The office was already busy. Barbie couldn't wait to help the children—and the doctor!

Barbie sat next to a girl with a purple cast. It was decorated with doodles.

"I like your cast," Barbie said.

"Thanks, but I'm getting it taken off today," the girl said. She looked worried. "I'm afraid it will hurt."

Barbie understood. She used to be scared to go to the doctor, too.

"Sometimes visiting the doctor can be scary when you don't know what to expect," said Barbie. "My friend Nikki had a cast. She said it tickled when the doctor took it off."

Nurse Mira called Barbie's name.

"Dr. Vargas is the nicest doctor ever," Barbie said to the girl. "When you're all done, she'll let you pick something special from her secret treasure box."

Nurse Mira smiled at Barbie. "It looks like you already have a good bedside manner," she said. "That's when you make patients feel comfortable. It's very important when you're a doctor."

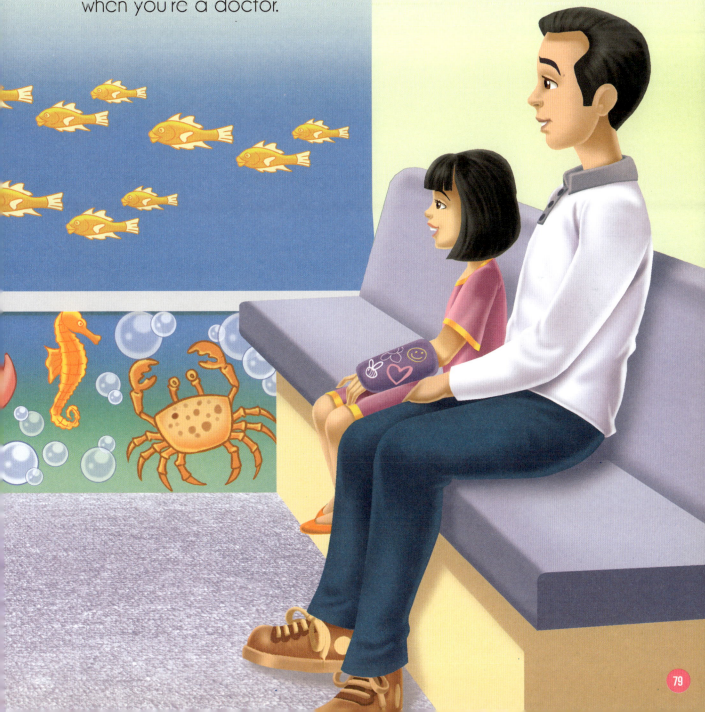

"Washing your hands before and after every patient is also very important," Nurse Mira said.

Barbie washed her hands while Nurse Mira pulled out a blue lab coat for her to wear. The blue lab coat meant Barbie was a volunteer.

"Why don't you help me until Dr. Vargas is ready?" asked Nurse Mira.

Nurse Mira and Barbie went into an exam room.
"Oliver is here for his well-child visit," said Nurse
Mira, handing Barbie Oliver's chart. "It's a checkup
to make sure he is healthy and strong."

Oliver stood on the scale, and Barbie entered
his weight in his chart. Mira checked her work and
nodded.

Next, Nurse Mira raised a slider on a measuring stick to the top of Oliver's head.

"Hmm, you seem very tall this morning, Oliver," said Nurse Mira. Oliver laughed, and Barbie saw he was standing on his tiptoes.

"Let's try with flat feet," said Nurse Mira. "Forty inches tall!"

Nurse Mira then checked Oliver's blood pressure. "This is so we know how strong your heart is," she explained.

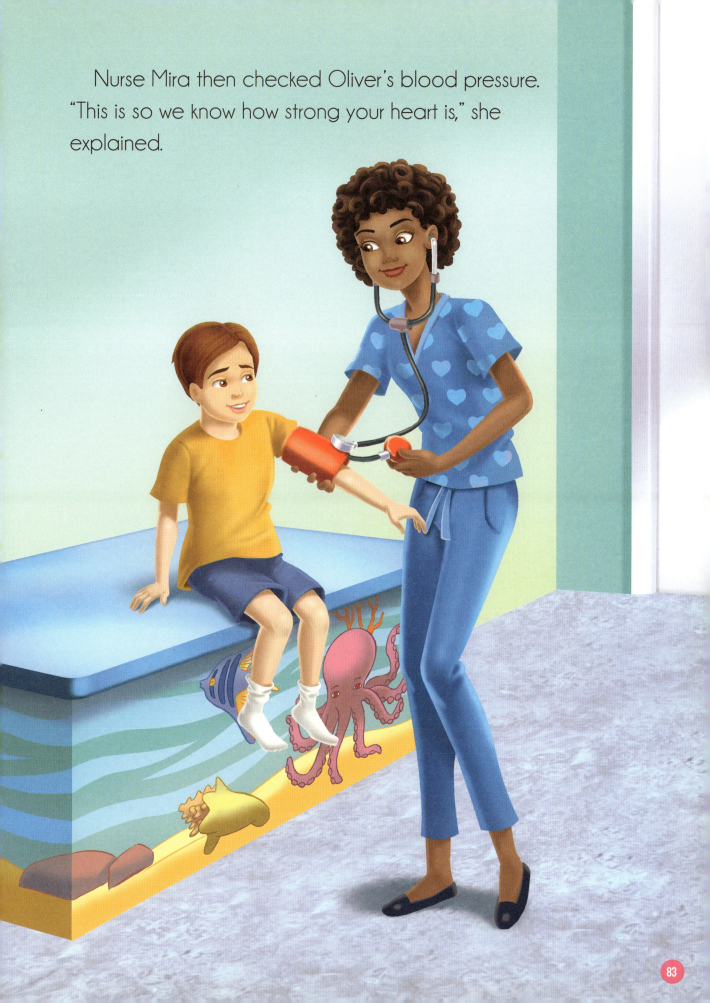

After each part of the exam, Barbie entered the
information into Oliver's chart. It was important to make
sure everything was correct. Dr. Vargas would use the
chart to review Oliver's progress.

Dr. Vargas entered the room and said hello to Barbie and Oliver.

"We have a few more things to check, Oliver," said Dr. Vargas. She looked in Oliver's ears with an otoscope.

"That tickles!" Oliver giggled.

Then she listened to his breathing with a stethoscope. He took two big, deep breaths.

Dr. Vargas looked over Barbie's notes on Oliver's chart. "Everything looks great, Oliver. You're healthy, happy, and ready to start first grade!"

"And I'll be even taller in second grade!" he said.

Oliver hopped down from the table and gave them each a high five on his way out.

In the next exam room, Barbie saw a familiar face.

"Barbie, this is Lily. She broke her arm," said Dr. Vargas.

"I met Lily earlier!" said Barbie with a smile. "She was really brave in the waiting room."

"We need to see if Lily's arm has healed," said Dr. Vargas.
"Barbie, can you please escort Lily and her father to the
X-ray room next door?"

"What does this do?" asked Lily. She was a little nervous.
"This machine uses a special light to make a picture of
your bones," said the X-ray technician. "That way we can
see inside your cast."

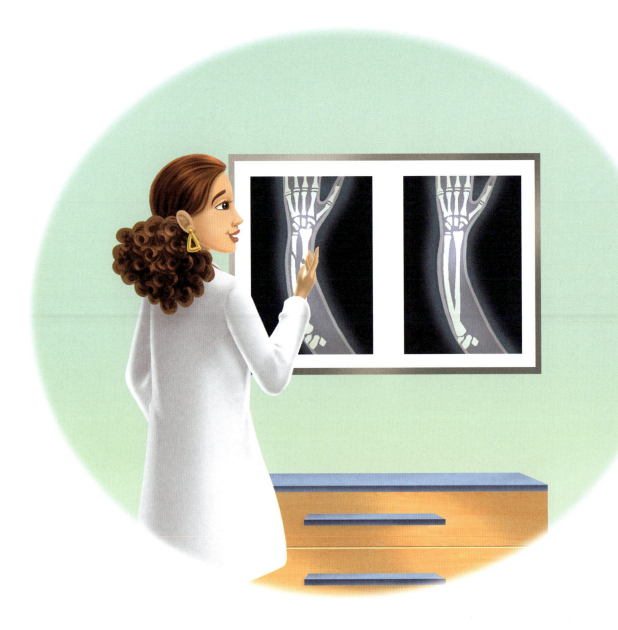

"This is the first X-ray of your broken arm," said
Dr. Vargas, pointing to a picture. "And this is the X-ray
we just took."

Barbie could see that the broken bone was
completely healed inside the cast.

"Does this mean Lily's cast will be removed today?"
asked Barbie.

"Yes. I just need to grab a few tools," said
Dr. Vargas, smiling.

Barbie could see that Lily was still nervous. "Remember what my friend told me?" she said. "It doesn't hurt—it just tickles. And I'll be here the whole time."

First, Dr. Vargas used a special cast saw that vibrated and cut the cast.

"It does tickle!" Lily laughed.

Next, Dr. Vargas used a cast spreader to separate the cast.

Then she let Barbie cut the padding with a pair of scissors.

"All done!" announced Dr. Vargas.

Lily flexed her fingers and waved her hand.

"Now you get to pick something from the secret treasure box!" said Dr. Vargas.

Lily was so happy! She chose a bright purple bouncy ball.

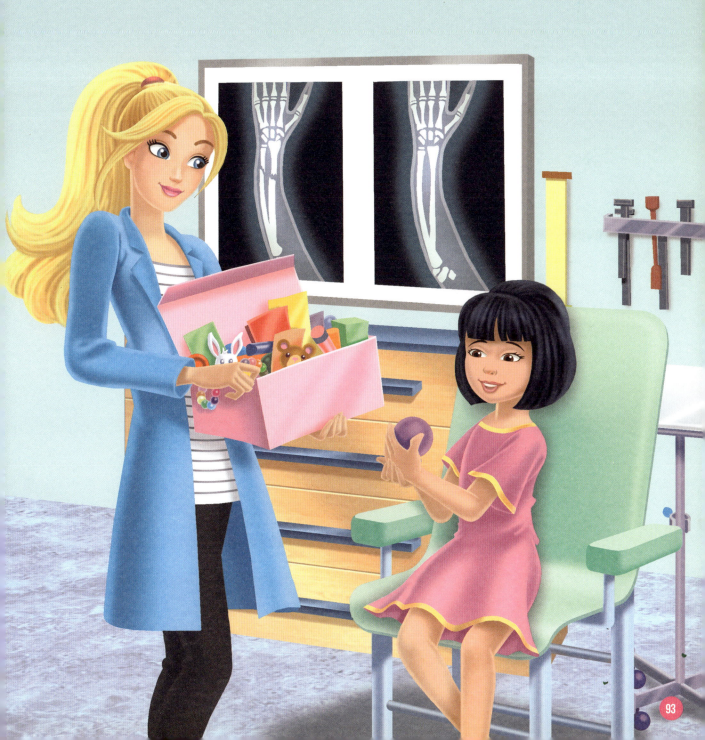

As Lily and her dad were leaving, a boy came
down the hall wearing a leg cast.
"Don't worry. It's not scary. Barbie and Dr. Vargas are
the nicest!" Lily said to the boy.

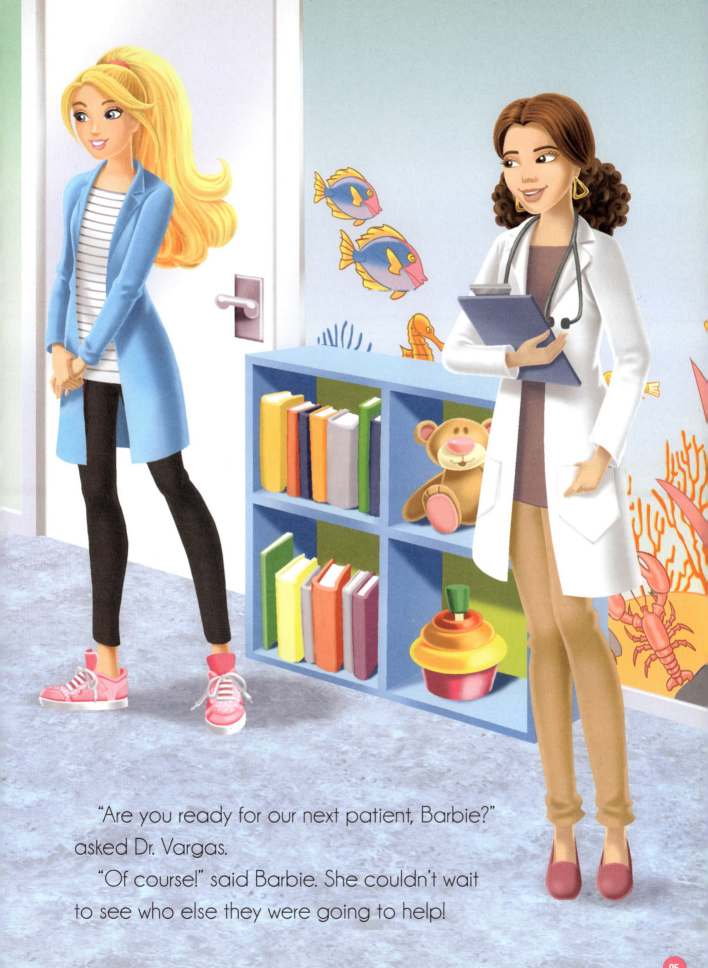

"Are you ready for our next patient, Barbie?"
asked Dr. Vargas.

"Of course!" said Barbie. She couldn't wait
to see who else they were going to help!

Dear Dr. Vargas and Nurse Mira,

Thank you for letting me volunteer with you! Seeing Lily be brave while her cast was removed was so cool. And I really liked taking notes on Oliver's chart. One day, I hope I can help people just like both of you do!

Your friend,
Barbie

It was a perfect morning. Barbie couldn't wait to ride her horse, Tawny. But when she got to the stables, they were closed!

"Oh no!" she cried.

Barbie had forgotten there was a horse show that day. She was disappointed, but she decided to stay and see the show.

Barbie sat in the stands and watched the riders walk, trot, canter, and jump with their horses. Each rider had a number pinned to her back. Judges made notes and kept score.

One rider on a gray horse jumped higher and moved more gracefully than all the others. She won first place! Barbie had never seen anyone ride like that.

Afterward, Barbie greeted the winning rider. "Hi, I'm Barbie," she said. "You were amazing!"

"Thank you," the rider said. "My name is Mandy, and this is Jade. She's like family."

"So is my horse, Tawny!" said Barbie.

"Have you and Tawny ever been in a horse show?" Mandy asked.

"No," said Barbie. "I'd love to be in a show onc day, but I'm not sure I'm good enough."

"I wasn't always a championship rider," Mandy said. "I practiced a lot. There's a show for beginners here at the stables in the fall. If you want to compete, I can help you prepare."

"That would be wonderful," Barbie said. "Thank you!"

Barbie and Mandy planned to meet back at the stables the following week.

"Are you and Tawny ready?" Mandy asked.

"Yes!" Barbie said with a huge smile.

The first thing she learned about was grooming.

"I love brushing Tawny's mane and tail to make them shiny and beautiful," Barbie said.

"Don't forget her hooves," Mandy reminded her. "They have to be clean, too."

Next, Mandy showed Barbie how to get her horse's tack ready for a show. Barbie cleaned Tawny's saddle and oiled the bridle. Then she shined the buckles until they sparkled.

"I know that the straps on the saddle have to be tight so it doesn't slip," Barbie said.

"Yes," Mandy said. "Safety always comes first, for both you and Tawny."

Then Mandy took Barbie to a riding store to buy show clothes. Barbie admired her new outfit in the mirror.

"I feel like a champion already!" she said.

The next day, Barbie and Tawny began practicing in the ring.

"Sit up straight, hold your hands low, and look in the direction you want your horse to turn," Mandy instructed Barbie.

Barbie and Tawny trained almost every day. Barbie learned the correct way to post, which means going up and down in the saddle in time with the horse's step. Then she learned to jump.

"Lean into it!" Mandy called.

Barbie and Tawny did it!

Later, Mandy said, "You need something to work toward."
"My goal is to learn all I can, become a better rider, and win one of the top three ribbons in the beginner competition," Barbie said, admiring Mandy's wall of awards.
Mandy nodded. "Those are great goals."

Finally, fall arrived. It was one week before the horse show. Mandy told Barbie she was ready, but it was time for Tawny to take a few days off to rest.

"You don't want to overwork your horse before the show," she said. "Horses need rest, just like people do."

The day before the show, Barbie was on her way to feed Tawny and ran into her friends Summer and Teresa.

"We're riding up to Oak Ridge for a picnic," Summer said. "Do you want to come?"

Barbie had been working hard for so long. A quick, easy ride wouldn't hurt, she thought.

"I'd love to go!" Barbie said.

The trail to Oak Ridge was a bit steeper and rockier than Barbie had remembered. Barbie looked at the valley below. "I can see the stables from here!"

The friends enjoyed a delicious picnic of sandwiches, fruit, and salad. They talked about what had happened during the summer.

"Did you know Steven started taking tuba lessons?"
Teresa asked. "He's pretty good!"

"And loud!" added Summer.

The girls laughed.

It was getting late. Barbie realized she'd better
get home and rest up for the show.

In the morning, Barbie was excited to ride in her first horse show! Mandy gave her some last-minute tips. "Walk a few laps around the ring to warm up and relax, and trust yourself."

But as Barbie led her horse toward the ring, she noticed Tawny was limping!

Barbie told Mandy about the trail ride and the picnic.

Mandy didn't think it was anything serious, but a veterinarian would have to look at Tawny's leg. In the meantime, Barbie and Tawny would not be able to ride in the horse show. Barbie felt terrible.

The vet told Barbie and Mandy that Tawny had bruised her foot. The horse would have to take it easy and stand on only soft ground for a while.

"I'll bandage it, and she'll be fine in a few weeks," the vet added.

"Will Tawny be well enough in time for next month's show?" Barbie asked.

"Absolutely!" the vet said.

Barbie took Tawny on slow, gentle walks around the
soft dirt in the ring. The horse's limp was gone in no time.
"You're a good girl, Tawny," Barbie told her horse.
"From now on, I'll make sure we're extra careful on the
trails and that we get plenty of rest before every show."

The night before the horse show, Barbie didn't take any chances.

"You're going to bed early, and so am I!" she said as she put a blanket over Tawny and said good night.

At the show, Barbie and Tawny were first in the ring for the warm-up. "I'm a little nervous," Barbie said.

"Well, I'm not," Mandy said. "You and Tawny will do great!"

"Thank you for all your help," Barbie said with a smile.

Soon it was Barbie and Tawny's turn. Barbie remembered everything Mandy had taught her. She sat up straight, held her hands low, and looked in the direction she wanted Tawny to turn. She leaned into her jumps just the way she had practiced.

When the show was over, Barbie had reached her goal—she had won a second-place trophy and a red ribbon for Tawny! She was one of the top riders!

"I'm so proud of you!" Mandy told Barbie.

"Thank you," Barbie said. "And I'm so proud of Tawny!"

Tawny let out a loud neigh.

Dear Mandy,

Thank you so much for teaching me all about riding in a horse show. You're the best! I learned about grooming, cleaning, and tack. I also learned how to use good riding form while riding Tawny, and how to set goals and meet them. My next goal is to win first place!

Your friend,
Barbie

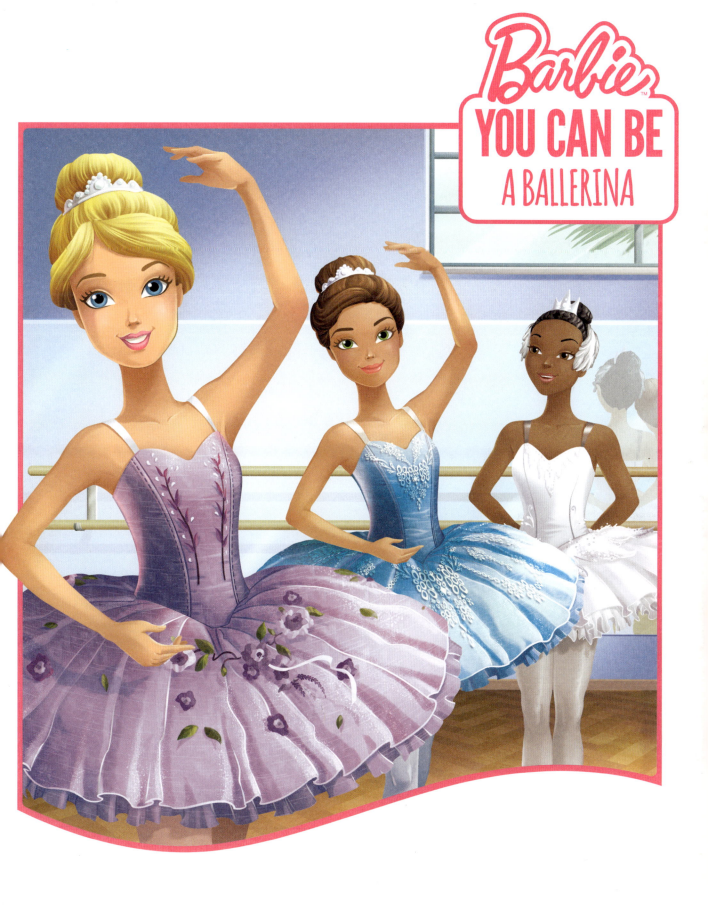

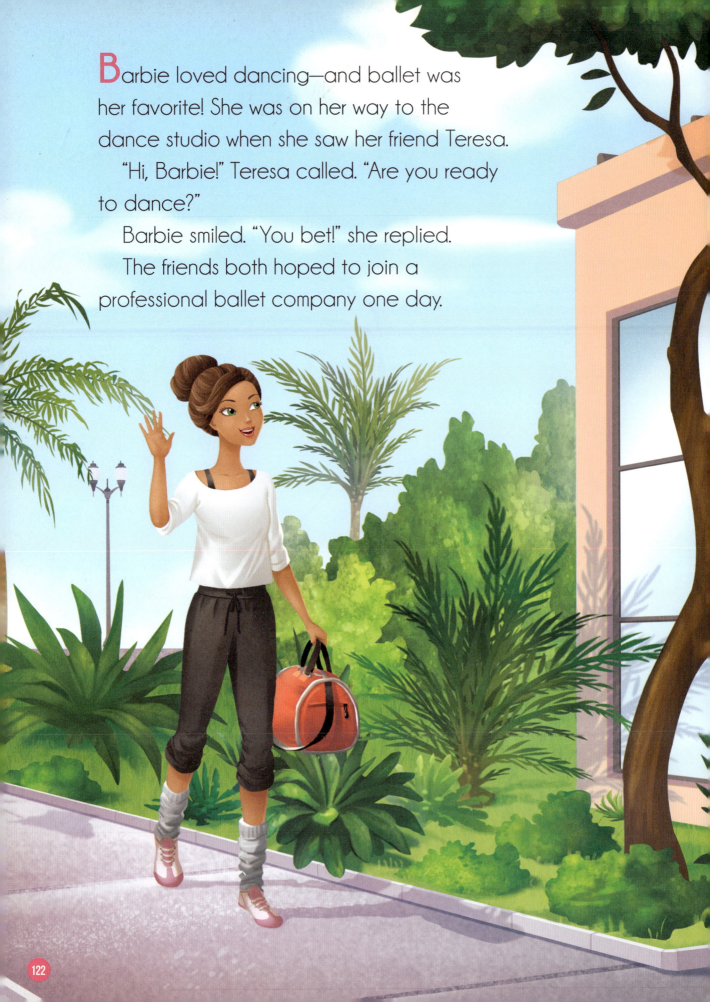

Barbie loved dancing—and ballet was her favorite! She was on her way to the dance studio when she saw her friend Teresa.

"Hi, Barbie!" Teresa called. "Are you ready to dance?"

Barbie smiled. "You bet!" she replied.

The friends both hoped to join a professional ballet company one day.

Barbie and Teresa joined the other dancers warming up for class. They stretched, and then they followed their teacher, Ms. Rita, through the ballet instructions.

Ms. Rita turned on the music, and the dancers moved gracefully across the floor.

Barbie first practiced a type of leap called a grand jeté.

Teresa stood on her toes in a position called relevé.
The dancers kept their backs straight and their
shoulders down as they moved their arms in the air.
"One, two, three, and four!" Ms. Rita called in time
with the music.

Then the dancers practiced their pirouettes. They had been working on the difficult turn for a while now. Teresa performed a graceful pirouette.

Barbie was next. She lifted her leg, but she lost her focus and nearly fell!

"Don't forget to practice spotting," Ms. Rita reminded her. Spotting is when dancers focus their eyes on one spot on the wall and quickly twist their heads to follow the spot.

"I will, Ms. Rita. Thank you!" replied Barbie. She knew that spotting was important for keeping her balance and not feeling dizzy.

Barbie was disappointed after practice.

"Let's work on our pirouettes together this week," said Teresa. "It will be fun!"

"That would be awesome," replied Barbie. "Thanks!"

Barbie and Teresa practiced and practiced their pirouettes. It took a lot of concentration to complete the move, but the two friends enjoyed working together.

At their next class, the friends performed the move again. This time both dancers completed graceful pirouettes! Ms. Rita was proud of them.

"Good work today!" Ms. Rita said at the end of class. "Barbie and Teresa, may I see you in my office?"

"Of course," Barbie said.

"I've noticed that you have both been working very hard, especially on your pirouettes," Ms. Rita said. "My colleagues at the city ballet company are performing tomorrow. Would you like to go?"

"We'd love to!" Teresa exclaimed.

"Thank you!" added Barbie.

The next morning, Barbie and Teresa went to the city ballet. They were introduced to a ballerina named Linda.

"I hear you two would like to dance professionally someday," Linda said. "Let's start by meeting some of the dancers. Then you can see what a professional dancer's life is like."

"This is Carly, and this is Mike," Linda said to Barbie and Teresa. "They are two of our best dancers."

"It's nice to meet you both," Carly said. "Would you like to dance with us during our practice today?"

"Sure!" Barbie said.

"This is our dressing room," Linda explained. "It's not very fancy, but it works for us!"

Barbie and Teresa looked at the dressing tables and the colorful costumes lined up on racks.

"Costumes and makeup help our ballerinas get into character," Linda explained.

Barbie and Teresa followed Linda to the morning dance class.

"Even professional ballerinas practice a lot," Linda explained. "Right now everyone is warming up."

"Do you have a teacher?" asked Barbie.

"Of course!" Linda said. "We never outgrow our teachers. She'll be here soon."

When the teacher arrived, she had the class practice leaps.

Barbie was nervous, but she did her best. When the teacher asked the dancers to practice a difficult leap, Barbie remembered what she had learned in her own class and performed it beautifully.

After class, Linda told Barbie and Teresa that the company needed two more background dancers for the performance. "Would you like to join us?" she asked. Barbie and Teresa were thrilled!

Backstage, the costume designer helped Barbie
and Teresa get ready. Barbie loved her outfit.

When everyone was dressed and ready, the
stage manager told them to take their places.
Barbie and Teresa wished each other good luck.